The Mystery
of the Missing Tiger

**Join Jen and Zeke
in these other exciting
Mystic Lighthouse Mysteries!**

The Mystery of
Dead Man's Curve

The Mystery of
the Dark Lighthouse

The Mystery of
the Bad Luck Curse

Coming Soon:

The Mystery of
the Phantom Ship

The Mystery
of the Missing Tiger

Laura E. Williams

SCHOLASTIC INC.

New York Toronto London Auckland Sydney
Mexico City New Delhi Hong Kong

For Sheryl, John, Matt, and Josh

A Roundtable Press Book

For Roundtable Press, Inc.:
Directors: Julie Merberg, Marsha Melnick, Susan E. Meyer
Project Editor: Meredith Wolf Schizer
Computer Production: Carrie Glidden
Designer: Elissa Stein
Illustrator: Laura Maestro

ISBN 0-439-21728-8

12 11 10 9 8 7 6 5 4 3 2   2 3 4 5 6/0

Printed in the U.S.A.
First Scholastic printing, March 2001

Contents

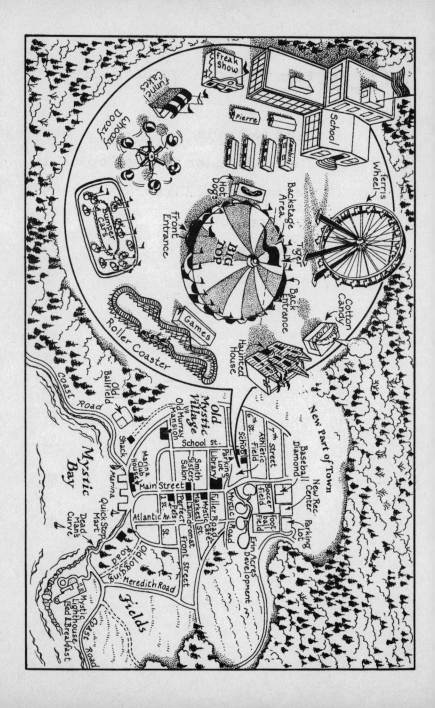

Note to Reader

   Welcome to *The Mystery of the Missing Tiger*, where YOU solve the mystery. As you read, look for clues pointing to the guilty person. There is a blank suspect sheet in the back of this book. You can copy it to keep track of the clues you find throughout the story. It is the same as the suspect sheets that Jen and Zeke will use later in the story when they try to solve the mystery. Can you solve *The Mystery of the Missing Tiger* before they do?

Good luck!

Disaster Under the Big Top

"This is so cool!" Jen exclaimed, nudging her best friend Stacey in the ribs. She'd never been to a circus before and didn't know where to look first. Fresh Maine air wafted through the open flaps of the red-and-white-striped big-top tent. Sitting in the fifth row with her twin brother, Zeke, and their best friends Stacey and Tommy, Jen had a great view of the dusty ring in the center of the tent.

Zeke checked his watch. The show wouldn't start for another ten minutes. "Good thing we got here early," he commented as more and more laughing people crowded into the big top. He saw groups of kids from school and waved. Little kids ran in, their faces buried in big pink puffs of cotton candy. Their parents hurried in after them.

Jen nodded. "We lucked out getting the circus

right here at Mystic Middle School. I'll bet all the high school kids are bummed that they had to rush over after school from the other side of town!"

Stacey stood up to stretch out her leg.

"What's wrong?" Jen asked.

Stacey grimaced and leaned down to massage her plump calf. Her short, curly blond hair fell forward. "I think I pulled a muscle at yesterday's game when I jumped up to block that ball."

"It was a great save," Jen said. "We won because of you." Now their soccer team, the Mystic Monsters, would go on to the playoffs.

Stacey sat down and tenderly rubbed her leg. "I just hope I can play by next week. I don't want to miss the first game at the new field." Yesterday's game was the last that would be played at the old recreational field. From now on, all the teams would get to play at the brand-new ballfield. The awesome new clubhouse even had showers and an indoor pool. The old field only had a beat-up old shack that barely protected the equipment from rain.

"Just think, we've lost our last ball to the Atlantic Ocean," Jen added, remembering how she had kicked the soccer ball over the fence yesterday, sending it rolling over the cliff and down to the ocean below.

"And now we'll be able to hear Coach Riley's

instructions!" Stacey said, her light blue eyes sparkling.

Jen laughed. The only thing louder than Coach Riley's voice was the sound of the ocean crashing right near the old field. You couldn't hear anything on days when the ocean was whipped into a frenzy by a coming storm or an especially strong wind. It was about time the Mystic recreation department built a new field and clubhouse.

Zeke leaned forward and pointed toward the ring. "Look, they're gonna start."

The crowd cheered as three clowns tumbled into the ring, pushing each other and then somersaulting out of each other's way.

"That one looks like a kid," Jen said, pointing to the shortest clown. He wore a blue-and-green polka-dotted clown suit, and his bright green hair stuck out in tufts all over his head. A huge smile was painted on his face, and his nose was covered by a red-and-blue ball.

The boy clown jumped forward onto his hands and walked around the entire ring while the other clowns playfully somersaulted and cartwheeled in his way. When he stood up again, the audience clapped wildly.

Five jugglers ran into the ring, their bright yellow-and-black costumes making them look like buzzing bees. They were tossing fluorescent pink balls around and around and back and forth at a dizzying rate.

"And I thought *I* was good with a soccer ball," Jen said with a sigh of admiration. She could keep a ball in the air for a long time, bouncing it with her head, knees, and ankles, but these jugglers were truly amazing. "I guess I can't join the circus."

Zeke laughed. "Don't feel bad," he said. "Aunt Bee would never let you go, anyway. Who would help me clean the bed and breakfast?"

Jen smiled. They had been living with Aunt Bee ever since their parents' death when the twins were just two years old. Aunt Bee, their grandmother's sister, had become like a parent to them. Living in the Mystic Lighthouse B&B was perfect. The twins got to live in the remodeled lighthouse tower, and they ate very well, since Aunt Bee was the best cook in town.

Suddenly, the crowd hushed. A tall, bald man with an enormous, glossy black handlebar mustache marched into the spotlight.

"Welcome! Welcome! WELCOME!" he said as he turned in a full circle. "I am Pierre the Magnificent, and I welcome you to my circus—the Most Amazing Show on Earth!" He lowered his voice. "Or at least in Maine," he added in a loud whisper.

The crowd laughed.

"We have a fabulous show for you this afternoon.

4

Sights you have never imagined! Animals tha
behave like humans! The Great Zambinis, who fly
through the air with the greatest of ease!" He held up
his hands to stop the applause. "But you must all
come back on Friday night . . ." He paused. "To see
Terra the tiger trainer in action with our new, our
very own, very special, and very rare Siberian tiger!"

A golden-haired woman wearing a black leotard
and sparkling tights ran into the ring. She was as tall
as Pierre and very thin. When she bowed in their
direction, Jen noticed she had catlike eyes. Terra
clawed the air with her bloodred fingernails, and her
mouth pulled back into a snarl.

"She looks even more fierce than a tiger," Stacey
whispered to Jen.

Jen nodded. She wouldn't want to mess with the
Siberian tiger . . . or its trainer!

As soon as Terra took her bows and ran out of the
ring, Pierre announced the first act. "Please welcome
Patti's Prancing Ponies!"

Everyone cheered as six adorable, ginger-colored
ponies circled the ring, tossing the bells on their fluffy
manes in time to the music. Jen didn't know where
the next hour went. One after another, varied acts
impressed and amused the crowd. After the ponies
came trumpeting elephants, ostriches that flipped

s back and forth over a net, and then made a human tower that was ten men n the acts, the clowns entertained the with their silliness. There were at least seven different clowns, and two of them were obviously kids around Jen and Zeke's age.

Jen looked around at the audience. The crowd was enthralled—laughing and clapping and pointing to things all over the ring. About five rows behind her, Jen noticed Mrs. Watson—Jen and Zeke's science teacher at Mystic Middle School—with her plastic pocketbook in her lap. Everyone knew Mrs. Watson was a strict vegetarian, and she used no animal products. She had once told Jen that even her hair dye was all natural and had never been tested on animals—which is why the color didn't always come out as planned. Right now it looked sort of greenish.

Jen waved, trying to get her teacher's attention. But Mrs. Watson sat stiffly, staring down into the ring with her face set as still as stone into a fierce frown. This was unusual—Mrs. Watson was good at telling jokes, and she liked to have a good time. She made science class fun by creating all kinds of neat experiments. Jen gave up trying to get her teacher's attention, but wondered why Mrs. Watson was the only person in the audience who wasn't having fun.

A drumroll sounded. Pierre the Magnificent moved to the center of the ring and held out his hands for quiet. When he finally got it, he announced, "And now the finale . . . the Greeeeeaaat Zambini Family!"

Spotlights focused on two poles at opposite sides of the ring that reached nearly to the top of the tent. A man and a teenage boy climbed up the pole on one side of the ring, while a woman and a girl who looked slightly younger than the boy climbed up on the other.

"I'm getting dizzy just watching them. I hope no one falls," Stacey whispered.

"They're trained for this," Jen said, craning her neck to watch the trapeze artists. She barely noticed that a safety net was spread across the ring in case one of them did fall. The Zambinis arranged themselves on the tiny platforms at the top of each pole. The father and mother simultaneously untied trapezes that had been secured near the platforms with ropes. The man handed the tiny swing—really just a bar suspended between two long ropes—to the teenage boy by his side, while the woman passed her trapeze over to the girl.

The drumroll stopped abruptly and was replaced by gentle, melodic music over the loudspeakers. The girl and the boy swung back and forth. The boy hung upside down and hooked his legs over the bar. Jen gasped as the girl let go of her bar in mid-swing, twirled through the air, and caught the boy's outstretched arms. It looked almost effortless, but Jen couldn't breathe again until each of them was standing on a platform, bowing to the wildly excited audience below them.

Mr. Zambini grabbed a different swing and swung out over the center of the ring. He locked his legs and ankles over the bar and pumped his arms so he went higher and higher with each swing.

The next thing happened so fast that Zeke wasn't sure he was seeing correctly. Then he heard a loud cry from everyone around him. One of Mr. Zambini's ropes had broken and he was plunging to the ground!

Searching for Clues

Zeke jumped to his feet and watched, horrified, as Mr. Zambini fell into the net below.

"Oh no!" Jen gasped, trying to see over the heads of everyone standing up in front of her. "Is he hurt?"

Pierre rushed into the ring, along with several of the clowns. They helped Mr. Zambini off the net and onto his feet. The crowd erupted into applause when Mr. Zambini waved to the fans and limped out of the ring. Pierre remained behind to announce that tonight's circus would be canceled, but reminded everyone to return for Friday's show. "In the meantime, enjoy the rides outside!"

"Mr. Zambini could have been killed if that net hadn't been there," Tommy said after Pierre hurried out of the ring. He ran a hand over his buzzed brown hair. "I can't believe he didn't break an arm or leg."

"Or his head," Zeke added. "That was a really lucky fall."

Jen tightened her lips. "Or unlucky, depending on how you look at it."

The twins glanced at each other. They had seen enough strange occurrences before to wonder if this accident had anything to do with luck at all.

"Let's go see if Mr. Zambini is okay," Zeke suggested casually.

Tommy lifted his eyebrows at his friend. "You can't fool me, Dale," he said, using the twins' last name. "You're snooping. Well, I hate to disappoint you, but this was obviously just an accident. No mystery here."

Zeke shrugged. "You're probably right." Then he grinned. "But it can't hurt to look, right?"

Tommy rolled his brown eyes. "I'm not wasting my time looking for nonexistent clues. I'm hungry. Anyone want to go eat?"

The twins shook their heads, and Stacey said, "I have to get a story about the Zambini family for the school paper. This will definitely make the front page." She started down the bleachers. "I'll find you when I'm done," she called over her shoulder.

With a wave, Tommy joined the crowd heading

out of the tent. Jen and Zeke hopped over the seats to the ground level and headed backstage.

The area behind the ring was chaotic with performers milling around in their glitzy costumes, mixing with several people who looked as out of place as Jen and Zeke felt.

Jen caught sight of Stacey trying to push through the crowd surrounding the Zambinis, her notebook and pen in hand.

Zeke pulled Jen back as she started to follow her friend. "Let's wait till the crowd dies down a bit."

Jen nodded. They backed out of the way until they came up against some metal bars. Jen turned around to see what had stopped their backward progress and almost screamed. Instead, she caught her breath and grabbed Zeke's arm.

Zeke felt the alarm in Jen's grip and turned to look behind him. They were face-to-face with the huge head of the white Siberian tiger! The tiger was absolutely enormous.

"Good kitty," he mumbled, taking a hasty step away. "Good kitty!"

The tiger opened its mouth as if to yawn, but suddenly a tremendous roar bellowed out from deep in its chest. Jen stumbled back in shock. The tiger licked its lips, blinked twice, then took three turns around the cage. Its muscles rippled gracefully with each step. Jen knew it could take her head off with one bite if given the chance. She shivered. Thank goodness it was behind steel bars!

Terra rushed over, her green eyes flashing. "Lady," she crooned. "Hush, Lady." She stuck her arm between the bars and scratched the tiger's massive head.

Jen and Zeke hurried away. When they were a safe distance from the cage, Zeke felt calmer. "I think I'd be a pretty good tiger trainer," he told his sister.

Jen lifted one eyebrow, something she had been practicing for months now. "Oh, really? Maybe after your knees stopped shaking."

Pierre's loud voice cut through the noise of the crowd. The twins turned to look. "Get out of here," the circus owner barked at a woman, his bald head wrinkled and red with anger.

Jen thought she recognized the odd, green cast to the woman's hair. Sure enough, when she turned, Jen saw it was their science teacher, Mrs. Watson. What was she doing back here, and why was Pierre so upset about it? Before Jen had a chance to find out, Mrs. Watson ducked out of sight.

Zeke pulled Jen behind another cage, grateful to see it wasn't filled with anything kid-eating, just two chattering monkeys. "Don't let Pierre see you," he warned. "We don't want to get kicked out of here before we have a chance to look around."

They watched Pierre head toward the tiger cage, where he confronted Terra about something. The twins were too far away to hear their conversation clearly over all the commotion backstage. Zeke edged forward, trying to stay partially hidden at the same time.

"You have to trust me," Terra said, a sharp edge to her voice. Her greenish cat eyes narrowed. "Trust me."

Pierre tugged nervously on one side of his mustache. "But everything depends on you. You have to pull this off, especially after what happened tonight, or we'll be ruined."

Terra scowled, looking fiercer than ever. "Don't worry, I've got it all planned. You'll get your money."

"I'd better!" With that, Pierre hurried away.

"What was that all about?" Jen asked Zeke when they had wormed their way through the crowd to avoid being seen by Pierre.

Zeke shrugged. "It sure didn't sound good, that's all I know."

Now that the crowd was thinning, Stacey had finally gotten through to the trapeze artists. Jen and Zeke heard Stacey's high, clear voice over the sounds of all the rides and amusements outside.

"Mr. Zambini, are you all right?" Stacey asked.

Jen and Zeke craned their necks to watch their friend in action.

Mr. Zambini nodded. "No problem," he said. He had a slightly foreign accent. "My leg is a little sore, but I'll go to the doctor tomorrow and everything will be fine."

Stacey scribbled something on her pad. Then she looked up again. "What happened to the rope?"

Mr. Zambini looked rueful. "I did not check it as I should have. It must have been frayed from overuse. I am just thankful that my dear wife and children were not injured." He hugged his wife to his side.

Stacey continued her questions. "How do you feel about Terra and her tiger taking over the spotlight of the show?"

Mr. Zambini's face turned red and for a split second contorted into an angry mask. But he regained control of himself and smiled thinly. "That is also no problem. The Great Zambinis are just that—great! Nothing can be greater! No more questions."

By now, the worried onlookers had left, and the backstage area was almost deserted. A couple of clowns were still chatting off to the side, and Zeke noticed a portly man standing in the shadows. He couldn't be sure, but it looked as if the man was wearing a fancy suit with a vest and watch chain over his rounded belly. When he raised his right hand to shoo away a bug, Zeke saw a flash of glittering diamonds on his pinky.

"Come on," Jen said, distracting Zeke for a second. When he looked back, the stranger was gone.

Zeke headed toward the exit, managing to pass as close to the Zambini family as possible.

"When William hears about this, he'll be worried," Mrs. Zambini fretted, her eyes red and her long, thin nose sniffling back tears. The two children had their mother's nose and their father's pointy chin.

Mr. Zambini put a hand on his wife's shoulder. "Call him, then, if it makes you feel better." He lowered his voice. "And tell him not to worry about the tuition money."

Jen poked Zeke in the back and urged him along faster. As they shuffled toward the exit, they caught sight of Mrs. Watson, who seemed to be trying to linger in the shadows without being seen while edging toward the tiger cage.

"What's she doing?" Jen asked Zeke.

"Let's go ask her," he suggested.

But at that moment, Mrs. Watson looked over at the twins. She frowned and disappeared behind several cartons of corn kernels that were obviously being stored there for the popcorn machine.

"Why is she avoiding us?" Jen said, about to head after their science teacher.

Zeke held her back and motioned behind them with his head. "Maybe she was looking at him, not us."

Jen turned and gulped. Pierre was headed right for them, a dark scowl on his face.

Nothing but Air!

The twins didn't wait for Pierre to reach them; they scurried out of sight as quickly as possible, ignoring Pierre's shouts commanding them to stop. Out of breath, they finally edged out of the big top. The sun had set, and the lights from the rides and games sparkled and shimmered.

"There's Mrs. Watson," Jen said, pointing. "Let's see what she was doing."

They followed her, trying to catch up, but the crowds kept getting in the way. When they reached a large circle of people watching an informal clown act near the cotton candy booth, they lost her for good.

"We'll have to ask her tomorrow in class," Jen said. "She was probably nosing around like we were." Then she smiled. "Or maybe she wants to join the circus."

Zeke laughed, but shook his head. "I don't think

so. Anyway, we haven't figured out what happened to Mr. Zambini's rope yet. I don't believe it was an accident."

"Let's go back into the ring," Jen suggested. "Maybe there's a clue there."

They sneaked around to the front entrance of the big top, afraid Pierre would jump out at them any second and demand to know what they were doing.

"The coast is clear," Zeke whispered.

The twins ducked into the big tent. The deserted ring looked a bit spooky now that the spotlight was off and the other lights had been dimmed. High above them, the trapeze towers disappeared into the darkness.

The large blue flap covering the entrance to the backstage area fluttered occasionally, but no one came through as Zeke and Jen quietly made their way into the ring. The sawdust covering the ground muffled their footsteps. They went around the ring in opposite directions, scouting around for clues. Jen found a tassel from one of the prancing ponies, and one of the jugglers' pink balls, but that was all.

"Find anything?" Jen whispered when she and Zeke met up on the other side of the ring.

Zeke shook his head. "Something that might have been elephant droppings," he whispered with a slight scowl, "but that's it. Seems like this is a waste of time. We may as well enjoy a couple of rides before Aunt Bee picks us up."

Jen shook her head, looking up. "I have an idea."

Zeke followed her over to one of the trapeze towers. "What are you doing?"

Jen put her hand on the first rung of the ladder-like steps that ran right up the pole. "If I go up there, I might be able to inspect the rope."

"Are you crazy?" Zeke exclaimed, forgetting to keep his voice down. Just looking up the pole made him dizzy. "Just because you can climb a tree like a monkey doesn't mean you can climb this. You could get killed."

Jen didn't answer. The next thing Zeke knew, she was at least ten feet above him and climbing steadily. His hands were slick with sweat, watching her nervously from below. He wanted to shout, "Get down from there!" but he was afraid that any loud noise would startle her. There was no net on this side of the trapeze tower.

Jen tried not to think about how far away the ground was. "Hand, foot, hand, foot," she kept repeating. She kept her eyes straight ahead. If she looked down, she knew she would be doomed.

Luckily she was in great condition from all the

hours spent on the soccer and softball fields. But her nerves were eating away at her energy. She was worried that if she didn't make it to the top soon, her legs might give way.

Just as she was tempted to give up and head back down, her hand hit the platform. She carefully scrambled over the edge and rested for a long moment on her hands and knees.

"Are you okay?" Zeke's voice floated up to her.

She took a deep breath and peeked over the edge of the narrow platform. "I'm fine," she replied. Zeke was just a dark shadow about a million miles below her. She closed her eyes. *Don't look down*, she reminded herself.

Trying to calm her nerves, she slowly stood up. All the trapeze ropes had been gathered and tied together and attached to the pole. Keeping one hand on the small handle jutting out from the post, she leaned forward and grabbed the ropes, trying to tug them closer to her. They swung a little, but not close enough for her to examine them. She realized she'd have to let go of her handhold.

Was the post swaying, or was that her imagination? *Get a grip*, she told herself firmly. She edged closer to the ropes, reluctantly letting go of the pole. Gingerly, she grabbed hold of the broken rope and

examined it closely. This was no accident—the rope had been cut!

"Hey!" someone shouted from below.

Jen jumped in alarm. Her foot slipped. She lunged wildly for the ropes, the post, anything to grab onto, but all she felt was air rushing past all around her!

Sabotage

Jen tried to scream, but the sound got stuck in her throat. She tumbled through the air, falling . . . falling. . . . Instinctively she twisted and curled into a ball just in time. She landed on the net, which felt like a very large trampoline. When she stopped bouncing, she scrambled to the edge of the net, leaned over and grabbed the underside, then flipped over and off of it, landing gracefully on solid ground.

Zeke grabbed her in a bear hug. "I thought you were a pancake."

Jen hugged him back. "So did I," she admitted with a shaky laugh. "Who was the jerk who yelled?"

"I was," said a boy clown wearing a polka-dotted suit, with a big smile still painted on his face. But Jen could see that under his makeup, he was frowning.

"What do you think you were doing up there?" the boy demanded.

Jen felt her spine stiffen. "I was just checking something out. Who are you, anyway?"

The clown boy narrowed his eyes. "Checking something out?" he asked doubtfully. "Not trying to cut the ropes?"

"No way!" Jen exclaimed.

"We'd never do that," Zeke said before his twin could say something she'd regret later. She had a bad habit of putting her foot in her mouth. "We just want to know what's going on."

The clown relaxed and he grinned. "Sorry about that," he apologized. "I guess I'm kind of upset about Mr. Zambini's accident." The clown turned to Jen. "I'm really sorry for scaring you. I thought maybe someone was up to no good. I'm glad you're okay. Oh, and my name's Mitchell, by the way."

The twins introduced themselves, both wondering if Mitchell could be trusted.

"I thought maybe the rope was cut or something because some strange stuff has been happening lately," Mitchell admitted. "When I saw you up there, the first thing that ran through my head was that the jerk who did it was back. I'm really sorry."

Jen waved away his apology. "Don't worry about it. You were just trying to protect the circus." She looked at Zeke and he nodded. "And you were right about the vandalism. Before I fell I saw the rope. Someone cut through it with a knife. Only a little edge of it was frayed. Also, I noticed some masking tape on the rope, as though whoever had cut the rope left a little still attached, then covered their work with the tape to disguise it."

"So none of the Zambinis would have noticed it when they got up there," Zeke added.

Jen nodded. "Exactly. And they were so involved with the audience, they obviously wouldn't notice it later, either. Not until it was too late."

Mitchell shuddered, his big blue-and-red nose wobbling on his face. "Who would want to ruin our show like that?"

"That's exactly what we want to find out," Zeke answered. "Do you know anyone who would want to hurt the Zambinis?"

"But it's not only the Zambinis," Mitchell said quickly. With crossed eyes, he pointed to his nose. "Look at this. It used to be red, but right before the show someone splattered blue paint over all the clown noses in the dressing room."

"That's not exactly as bad as cutting a trapeze

rope," Jen pointed out.

Mitchell frowned. "It may not seem like much to you, but clowns are very particular about their noses. And costumes have disappeared. Also, the other day the ostrich trainer found a metal spike in the ostrich cage. Luckily none of the birds got hurt."

"Someone is definitely trying to damage the circus," Zeke said thoughtfully. "We didn't find any clues here, but maybe we should check out the dressing room. You said stuff has been happening there, too."

"Sure," Mitchell said, leading the way. "I'll show you. I've worked and traveled with the circus all my life. My parents are two of the jugglers. I don't know what we'd do if Pierre closed down the show."

"Maybe we'll be able to help," Jen said. She didn't tell Mitchell that they had successfully solved other mysteries. She didn't want to raise his hopes, just in case.

The clowns' dressing room was a long trailer that had been painted on the outside with giant, smiling clown faces. Inside, it smelled like greasepaint, sweat, and dirty socks. All of the clowns were still in costume out on the grounds. Mitchell told them it was part of their job to entertain the crowds after a show until closing time. When the rides stopped at eleven P.M., there would be a mad rush in here with all seven clowns trying to remove their makeup at the same time. He waved his hands as he spoke, pointing out the dressing area and the brightly lit, mirrored makeup tables.

"What do you do about school?" Zeke asked.

Mitchell wrinkled his nose. "Don't worry, I can't get out of that. Pierre hired a teacher who travels with us and teaches all the kids. There are fourteen of us who live with the circus."

"Neat," Jen exclaimed.

Mitchell shrugged. "I guess it's pretty cool. But sometimes I wouldn't mind staying in one place longer than a week or a weekend. I'd like to live in a house for a month and see what it feels like."

"I guess that isn't so neat, after all," Jen said, changing her mind. She couldn't imagine not living at the B&B with Zeke and Aunt Bee.

"Anyway," Zeke interrupted, "where do you keep your noses?"

Mitchell pointed out the counter. Whoever had vandalized the noses had gotten blue paint on the countertop as well. "And we keep our costumes on this rack." He pointed. "We each have about four or five costumes because we sweat a lot in them and it's not good to wear the same one night after night." He swung a few hangers out to show them. "These are mine. I was the first to notice that one was missing. When we searched, we found several were gone. Everyone else thought the missing costumes were getting washed. But when we asked Jack, the man in charge of all the laundry, he said that he didn't have them."

"Who would want clown outfits?" Jen asked, amazed. Then she hastily added to Mitchell, "No offense."

Mitchell grinned. "You mean you wouldn't want to wear this to school?" He held out a red, white, and blue puffy one-piece suit and tapped his oversized shoe in pretend annoyance.

"Uh, it's very patriotic," Jen laughed. "Honestly, you wouldn't catch me dead in that—unless, of course, I was a clown."

Mitchell laughed, too. "Sometimes I do wear this to school . . . clown school!"

The twins warmed up to Mitchell, who straightened the rack of clothes. "These are old costumes," he said, pointing to several shoes and outfits at the end of the rack. "We wear out our costumes pretty quickly from jumping and rolling around, but sometimes it's hard to get rid of a favorite."

Jen nodded. "I have T-shirts like that. I can't bear to get rid of them, but Aunt Bee won't let me wear them anymore."

"None of this helps solve the mystery of who is trying to sabotage the circus," Zeke pointed out. "If we don't figure this out soon, the next accident could be even worse!"

5

A New Suspect

The next morning, Jen stuffed her books into her backpack. After the circus the night before, Aunt Bee had picked them up and driven them home. Jen and Zeke had spent the rest of the evening doing homework.

"Why can't teachers cancel homework when there's something this exciting going on in Mystic?" she asked Slinky, her Maine coon cat. Slinky just yawned.

"Thanks a lot," Jen said with a laugh. "You're sure a big help."

"Ready?" Zeke asked, peeking in her door.

Jen hoisted her backpack over her shoulder and followed her brother down to the kitchen where they each grabbed a homemade cranberry-almond muffin.

"We're riding our bikes to school," Jen reminded Aunt Bee.

Aunt Bee nodded, sipping her cinnamon tea. Her long gray hair wasn't in its usual braid, but hung loosely down her back. "Have a great day," she said with a smile.

Zeke jumped up and exclaimed, "Of course we will. Today's Friday!"

"Shhh," Aunt Bee hissed. "Mr. Richards, the guest who checked in yesterday, is on the parlor phone and he asked not to be disturbed. He was quite upset that the guest rooms didn't have phones in them."

"He doesn't have a cell phone?"

Aunt Bee shrugged. "Apparently not. But take a look at his car as you leave," she said with a twinkle in her blue eyes. "Just tiptoe out."

Zeke motioned for Jen to follow him. They could have left through the back door in the kitchen, but he wanted to get a glimpse of Mr. Richards.

They crept by the parlor, but all they saw was Mr. Richards's slicked-back, glossy black hair and his back.

"That's right," Mr. Richards said. "Buy all five of them. Can never have too many bucks."

The twins moved on. "He must be a banker," Jen whispered.

They went outside and around the side of the

B&B. Zeke whistled in amazement. "He's got lots of bucks all right," he said, pointing to a small green sports car in the parking lot. "That must have cost him a fortune."

"It looks like an insect," Jen remarked, mystified. "What is it?"

"It's a Lamborghini, and it's worth hundreds of thousands of dollars!"

The twins raced down the B&B's long driveway. Then they pedaled on the side of the road that led into town. A few cars sped by them. They had ridden for about five minutes when Jen spotted a large, white truck with a black triangle painted on the side that had pulled over to the side of the road. The truck was very clean. The front hood was up and a man was peering at the engine.

Zeke braked to a stop. "Need any help?" he asked.

The man looked up and smiled, showing off a gold front tooth. "I sure do, kid. Know anything about truck engines?"

Zeke shook his head. "I don't, but my friend's uncle does. He owns a garage down the road. We're going right by there and could tell him you need help."

The stranger nodded and glanced at his watch. "That would be great, kid. I really appreciate it. I'm already late."

Zeke smiled. "No problem."

Jen waved to the man as they headed off. As soon as they got to the garage owned by Tommy's uncle, they pulled in and Zeke relayed the message as promised.

Tommy's uncle, Burt, was a gruff man who wore oil-stained coveralls. He thanked them with a nod of his balding head. Jen knew he didn't like kids hanging around the garage, and she urged Zeke away as fast as she could. She knew that even though Tommy loved his uncle, he didn't get in Burt's way, either.

At last they pedaled onto the school grounds. The circus was already bustling with workers feeding animals, and jugglers in normal clothes practicing their moves. Zeke noticed that one clown was already in costume and walking with a slight limp. He saw that the tiger cage was completely covered by a gold cloth with tassels on the edges. He wondered if Mitchell was in school with his circus friends and the teacher Pierre had hired.

The bike rack stood near the front entrance of the school. Zeke parked his bike, not bothering to lock it up. Detective Wilson, a great friend and a retired police detective, had told them that in all the years he worked on the Mystic police force, not even one bicycle had ever been stolen.

Jen parked her bike next to Zeke's. "I wonder what's going on over there," she said, looking toward a cluster of trailers where circus workers had gathered.

"Someone's mad about something," Zeke said, hearing an angry voice. "Let's check it out before the bell rings."

They hurried through the gathering crowd until they stood in front of one of the trailers. From the outside, everything looked fine. But Pierre stood in the doorway, shouting angrily, his mustache jerking up and down with each word. Jen stared at the circus owner. He was covered with splotches of blue paint.

"It's ruined," Pierre shouted. "Everything in my trailer is ruined! Blue paint everywhere! When I catch the vandal, he will pay!"

Jen learned from the bearded woman standing next to her that Pierre had left his trailer early that morning, but when he'd gone back to get something, he'd found the destruction. "So many things are going wrong," the woman murmured, shaking her head.

Not able to help herself, Jen blurted out, "Is your beard real?"

The woman took a step forward. "Of course it is. Wanna pull it?"

"Uh, no thanks." With that, Jen tugged Zeke

aside and told him what the woman had said about the paint in the trailer. "It's definitely part of the mystery," Jen said. "And her beard is real. I asked her."

Zeke rolled his eyes. When would she learn to keep her mouth shut? "At least this wasn't a dangerous accident," Zeke said in reference to the vandalism. "But it sure made Pierre mad." Then he cocked his head to one side and Jen could practically see his sensitive ears perk up. "Oops, there's the bell. We'd better get to homeroom."

They rushed into the building, then split up to head for their different homerooms. Jen hustled and made it to her seat just as the late bell shrilled.

"Where were you?" Stacey asked, leaning toward her. "You weren't on the bus."

"Bikes," Jen said, catching her breath.

The morning announcements came over the loudspeaker; Jen sorted through her books, only half listening as a student talked about next week's lunch menu, the boy's baseball team, and the math team championships. As soon as the announcements ended, Jen stood up, ready to head to first period, but then the principal's voice clicked on.

"One more announcement," she said. "As a special treat, today will be a half-day for students and teachers. Classes will last only twenty minutes each and no lunch will be served. Have fun at the circus this afternoon!"

A cheer erupted in homeroom. Jen looked at Stacey, her mouth in a silent O. "I should tell Aunt Bee it's only a half-day. She knows we're staying after school for the rides, but I should let her know school's getting out early."

On the way to first period, she stopped in the office and borrowed the phone, but the B&B line was busy. It was busy after first period, too. And after second, and third, and fourth. Finally, at eleven o'clock, she got through.

"Who's been on the phone?" Jen exclaimed. "I've been calling you forever!"

Aunt Bee sighed. "It was Mr. Richards. He must have talked to every country on this planet at least twice."

Jen shook her head. "Jeez, if I spent that much time on the phone, you'd have it disconnected."

Aunt Bee laughed. "You've got that right. Now what's so urgent?"

Jen told her aunt about the shortened day, and Aunt Bee asked if they had enough money to buy lunch and still go on all the rides.

"Don't worry, I've got twenty bucks," Jen said, using Mr. Richards's term. She hung up and ran to science class.

Mrs. Watson nodded to her when Jen entered. Stacey had already told her that Jen was trying to call her aunt.

"As I was saying," Mrs. Watson continued, "it is horrible the way they have those poor circus animals locked up and trained to do those silly tricks."

"But they're fun to watch," someone piped up.

Mrs. Watson ran her fingers through her oddly colored hair. Today it had a bit of an orange tinge to it. "It's not fun, it's . . . it's agonizing."

None of the students said anything.

"Especially that poor Siberian tiger, trapped in a cage like that. It's supposed to be a wild animal. It should be free. In fact, I'd do anything to put it back into its own environment. Anything!"

Jen glanced back at her brother, who sat two rows behind her. They raised their dark eyebrows at each other. It wasn't unusual for one of them to know what the other was thinking—it was a twin thing, they'd decided long ago.

Anything? they both thought.

6

Escape!

When the bell rang at 12:16, everyone cheered. Jen and Stacey met Zeke and Tommy, and they made their way toward the rides and games along with every other middle schooler.

"Sheesh," Stacey grumbled, shaking her blond curls. "Are there enough people here?"

"Let's try the Ferris wheel," Jen suggested. "The line isn't very long."

Before they knew it, Jen and Stacey were sitting on a swaying bench, heading up into the big, blue sky. At first the ride kept stopping and starting as the other passengers got off and on. Finally, it smoothed out.

"Yikes," Stacey said, gripping the bar across her lap. "I didn't know this went so high."

Jen laughed. "But look at the view." They gazed in all directions. Mystic Village spread out at their feet.

Beyond the buildings they could see the fields and the dark forest. To the east they followed Main Street down to the Mystic Marina and Mystic Bay. The Atlantic looked calm and sparkly in the sunlight.

"Hey, there's the B&B," Jen said, pointing toward the lighthouse.

"And there's the old ballfield," Stacey said, nodding south. "It looks so lonely and deserted."

Jen looked around for the new town field and recreation center, pointing it out when she spotted it.

By the time the ride had stopped, the girls had found all the major landmarks. They got off the Ferris wheel before the boys, so they waited for Zeke and Tommy to join them.

"That was cool," Tommy said. "We could see everything."

But Zeke didn't want to stand around talking. "Come on," he said. "Something's wrong."

Jen looked around. "Where?"

"The big top," Zeke called over his shoulder, already heading in that direction. "I saw it from the Ferris wheel."

Jen raced after her brother, Stacey and Tommy close at her heels.

When they entered the backstage area, Jen gulped. The gold covering had been pulled off the tiger cage, and the cage was empty!

"Where's the tiger?" Tommy asked, a nervous tremor in his voice.

"Lady is gone!" Terra said, as though she'd heard Tommy's question. She stood with a group of policemen near the cage. "But how did she get out?"

One of the officers said, "Someone must have stolen her."

"But that's impossible," Terra insisted, narrowing her cat eyes. "I checked on her very early this morning and I'm sure I locked the cage. No one could have gotten in there."

The policeman shrugged. "Does anyone else have the keys?"

"No. . . ." Terra bit her lip. "Well, actually, I misplaced my keys yesterday."

"Then how did you get in the cage this morning?"

"I have a spare set," Terra admitted.

"Someone probably stole your keys," the officer said grimly.

Terra shook her head in disbelief. "But who would want to steal Lady?"

At that moment Pierre charged up to the group. He took one look at the empty tiger cage and exploded. "Where's my star? Where's my tiger?"

A policeman tried to calm Pierre down. "Don't

worry. We'll find the cat. There aren't too many places to hide a tiger in Mystic."

Pierre fumed. He whirled on Terra, gripped her arm and yanked her aside. "This is all your fault," he hissed under his breath.

Zeke wondered if anyone else could hear them. He strained to hear the rest.

"If you don't find that cat, you won't have a job here or anywhere else. I'll make sure of it!"

Terra, who had looked upset before, now narrowed her eyes at Pierre and pulled her arm free. *She looks like Slinky when Slinky is mad,* Jen thought. Stacey and Tommy seemed to be more interested in watching the policemen as they talked into their radios to the rest of the force, who were out looking for Lady.

"You said I could trust you," Pierre went on. "Is this part of your plan? *Now* where will the money come from?"

Terra said something too soft to hear.

Pierre glared at the tiger trainer. "I'd better!" He let go of Terra and looked around. "Zambini. I need the Zambinis. They're all I've got left now. Where are they?" When Mr. Zambini didn't come forward, Pierre looked even angrier.

Finally, a voice called out, "I think my father is at the doctor's getting his leg checked." The girl who stepped forward was Mr. Zambini's daughter, the youngest of the trapeze artists.

"When will he be back?" Pierre demanded, tugging on his mustache.

The girl shrugged. "You said we weren't performing tonight because Terra and Lady were doing an extra-long show for the grand opening of their act."

Pierre stamped his foot. "Disaster!" he shouted, flinging his hands into the air and looking at the sky. "All of this is a disaster!" He marched away without looking back.

7

A Clue in Blue

Stacey rushed off after Pierre, digging her notebook out of her bag at the same time. "I'm going to try to interview him," she shouted over her shoulder.

"Good luck," Tommy muttered. "I'd rather face a starving tiger than Pierre. Talking about starving, I'm really hungry. Food anyone?"

Jen and Zeke glanced at each other then shook their heads. "Not yet," Zeke said. "But you go eat. We'll find you later."

Tommy shrugged. "It's *your* stomachs." He jogged away toward a sign that read HOT DOGS, SOFT DRINKS, COTTON CANDY, FRIED BREAD.

"Or your stomachache," Jen added to herself. She liked junk food as much as the next person, but not if there was any chance of going on a fast ride after eating it.

A nearby policeman reported to Terra, "So far there's absolutely no sign of the tiger. No one's seen him—"

"Her," Terra corrected.

"Her, or heard her growl or anything. We have all of our staff on patrol, working overtime and extra duty. Don't worry, we'll find Lady. Now, if you don't mind coming down to the station with us, we'd like to fill out a report."

Terra looked nervous for a second, then she gave a small smile and agreed.

By now the crowd had dispersed. Jen and Zeke waited until no one was near the cage, then stepped cautiously inside it.

"I wonder who stole Terra's keys?" Jen asked.

Zeke frowned. "Do you think Terra really lost her keys, or was that just a cover-up? Remember how she told Pierre he would get the money last night? I wonder what that's all about?"

Jen scanned the inside of the cage, looking for clues. "It sure doesn't make her sound completely innocent. But then again, what money is Pierre talking about? If I wanted money from someone, I wouldn't go around yelling at her."

"Maybe it was just an act on Pierre's part," Zeke suggested. He squatted down to look more closely at the straw covering the bottom of the cage. "Jen! Come here!" he exclaimed, trying to keep his voice down.

Jen hurried over and bent low to look. "Blue paint! It's the same color as the clown noses."

"And the same color as the paint inside of Pierre's trailer," Zeke added. "It's definitely the same person behind all of this."

Jen tipped her head sideways. "Brush a little of that straw away."

Zeke brushed the straw away.

"Now brush that away over there," Jen continued. When Zeke did, they both gasped.

Zeke stood up for a better view. "Is that what I think it is?" he asked.

"If you're thinking it looks like the outline of a huge footprint, then you're thinking what I'm thinking."

Zeke nodded. "So either a giant did this, or someone else who wears big shoes."

"The clowns!"

"Exactly. Let's go find Mitchell."

The twins hurried through the fairgrounds to the trailer covered with clown faces. They knocked on the door and Mitchell opened it, already in costume.

"Hi, you guys," he said. He didn't look too happy.

"Is this a bad time?" Jen asked.

Mitchell shook his head. "Did you hear what happened to Lady?"

The twins nodded.

"Everyone's afraid that without his new star, Pierre will shut down the circus. We've been struggling for a

while, but Pierre was hoping the tiger would bring in new crowds."

Jen looked at Zeke. *So that explained the money he wanted. Or did it?*

Mitchell let them into the trailer. "He's actually just canceled tonight's performance because he can't find Mr. Zambini. His daughter said he's at the doctor's office. I guess he hurt his leg pretty bad when he fell last night." He slumped onto one of the dressing room chairs. "We're doomed."

"Not yet," Zeke said. "If Jen and I find the tiger, the circus will be okay, right?"

Mitchell looked back and forth at them. "Of course. But what can you two do?" he asked, waving his hands when he talked.

Jen grinned. "You mean, what *can't* we do!"

Mitchell seemed to catch on to their hopeful mood. "Can you walk around the ring on your hands?"

Jen's grin faded. "You got me on that one."

Laughing, Mitchell said, "Don't feel bad. It took lots of years and a whole bunch of knocks on the head to get the hang of it." Then he sobered. "But seriously, how do you think you'll find the tiger when the police haven't even found it yet?"

"We've already uncovered a clue that they missed," Zeke said. "We found a blue footprint in the straw that the police didn't see. We'll find out whose it was."

Mitchell scrunched his eyebrows together and waved his hand around. "How does that help?"

"The footprint was huge," Jen elaborated. "Like a clown's shoe. And the blue is the same color that was painted on your noses."

"So one of the clowns is trying to ruin the circus?" Mitchell asked. "I can't believe it."

"If we can find the shoe with blue paint on it, we'll know who is sabotaging everything and has the tiger," Jen said, already looking toward the lineup of clown shoes.

Mitchell jumped to his feet. The three of them turned over every pair of shoes.

"Here it is," Zeke crowed, holding up a large yellow shoe.

"That's weird," Mitchell said. As he shook his head, his green clown hair bounced back and forth.

"Weird?" Jen repeated. "Why?"

"No one wears those shoes anymore. It's like those costumes I showed you yesterday. Worn out, but not ready for the garbage. Those shoes used to belong to Petey, and he doesn't even work with this circus anymore."

Zeke frowned. "You're sure you haven't seen any

of the clowns wearing these shoes?"

"I'm sure." Mitchell's face fell. "So much for the clue."

"We may not know exactly who the person is," Jen said, trying to sound cheerful, "but we know it's someone who was wearing those clown shoes."

"I figure that the person first sabotaged Pierre's trailer and got paint on his—"

"Or her," Jen butted in.

"Shoe," Zeke continued, "then hurried to the tiger cage and stole Lady while everyone was distracted by Pierre's problem." He motioned to Jen. "We went over to Pierre's trailer before school, too, to see what had happened, remember? Someone could have been stealing the tiger and no one would have noticed."

Mitchell nodded thoughtfully. "It sure makes sense. So we have to be on the lookout for a clown who's not really a clown."

"Exactly," Jen agreed, realizing that this task sounded nearly impossible. But she refused to give up. Just then her stomach growled loudly. "Well, we missed lunch, and now it's almost dinnertime. We'd better hurry home or Aunt Bee will think we were eaten by the stolen tiger."

The twins said good-bye to Mitchell, retrieved their bikes, and headed home.

"Burt must have picked up that guy's broken-down truck," Zeke commented as they rode closer to the B&B.

"Yup, I noticed it at his garage when we passed it."

They pedaled on, panting heavily as they headed up the long hill to the B&B. The light was fading, and the sun lit up the top of the lighthouse tower. The rest of the B&B sat in shadows.

"Who's that?" Jen huffed, trying to talk and pedal uphill at the same time.

Zeke looked up, too out of breath to answer. Two figures were talking by the side door of the B&B. He couldn't tell who they were.

As they neared the door, Jen peered through the gathering dusk, trying to make out their faces. Something just didn't look right about them, as though they were trying to stay hidden. Just then one of the figures looked up and saw Jen and Zeke approaching. Jen felt certain it was a man. He slipped inside the B&B, leaving the other person alone.

The lone figure flashed them a quick grin as he hurried away on foot, heading down the driveway Jen and Zeke had just come up.

"That was the truck driver from this morning," Jen said when she'd caught her breath.

"Are you sure?" Zeke asked. He thought it was too

dark to be able to make out the guy's face.

"I'm positive," Jen said firmly. "I saw the flash of his gold tooth."

Zeke shook his head as he parked his bike. "What would the truck driver have to do with any of the guests at the B&B?" he wondered out loud.

"I don't know," Jen said, putting down her kickstand. "But they looked pretty suspicious."

The Perfect Plan

The twins hurried inside, hoping to catch a glimpse of the mysterious stranger, but when they got to the front foyer, a group of bird-watchers who were staying at the B&B were on their way out to dinner. It was impossible to tell who might have been outside a second ago.

Disappointed, they searched for Aunt Bee and found her in the parlor talking to a well-dressed man with shiny black hair. They recognized him from that morning as Mr. Richards. She beamed at them as they walked in.

"Children, this is Mr. Richards, one of our guests."

Mr. Richards stood up to shake hands with the twins. Zeke stared hard at the man. He'd seen Mr. Richards at the circus last night after Mr. Zambini's accident—the man in the fancy suit. Zeke checked out his pinky. Sure enough, Mr. Richards wore a diamond pinky ring that was in the shape of a pyramid.

"Good evening," Mr. Richards said pleasantly, patting his round stomach.

Jen almost felt like she was supposed to bow to this elegantly dressed man. She could tell his clothes were expensive. He sat down again and smiled.

"Mr. Richards was just telling me about fascinating places," Aunt Bee said. "He's traveled all over the world."

Jen noticed the man's briefcase at his feet for the first time. It was covered with travel stickers. It didn't exactly look like something a well-dressed businessman would carry around, but maybe he was eccentric. She peered closely at the stickers.

"You've been to all those places?" she asked. "South America," she read out loud, "Hawaii, the Amazon, Siberia, the Everglades, Africa." The rest of the stickers were partially covered or too small to read from a distance. "I've always wanted to go on a safari in Africa."

The man chuckled. "I've been on at least a dozen safaris there."

Jen was genuinely impressed. "Wow."

Zeke frowned. He couldn't imagine what this man

might be doing with a gold-toothed truck driver. But surely none of the bird-watchers had been talking to the truck driver. Zeke looked up as another man walked into the parlor.

"Is your room comfortable?" Aunt Bee asked the tall man.

Zeke was surprised to see Pierre the Magnificent.

"It's fine," Pierre grumbled. "Too many flowers for my taste," he added with a scowl as he saw the twins.

Jen hid a laugh. Her aunt was used to cranky guests and never got upset no matter how rude they were. "Well, your trailer will be cleaned in no time, and you'll be able to go back to it," said Aunt Bee soothingly.

"Just another added cost," he mumbled. "Had to cancel tonight's show. Do you know how much money I'm losing? Lots. Lots and lots," he stressed. "And now with Lady missing." He shook his head in disgust. "The star of our show gone." Suddenly, he brightened a little. "But thank goodness for the Big Top Insurance Company."

Jen and Zeke looked at each other.

"I'm hitting the hay," Pierre continued. "Circus life starts before the sun is up. G'night." Abruptly he turned away and stomped out of the parlor.

Aunt Bee shrugged. "The poor man is not having a very good time of it. I hope everything works out for him."

Mr. Richards nodded in agreement.

The twins excused themselves and Aunt Bee told them dinner would be ready in about a half hour. They headed up to Jen's room to talk. Each of the twins had a bedroom and a bathroom in the light-house tower. Aunt Bee's husband, Uncle Cliff, had renovated it, creating Jen's room on the second floor and Zeke's on the third. A spiral staircase ran from the lighthouse museum on the first floor, past the bedrooms, all the way up to the light itself. Unfortunately, Uncle Cliff died just before the grand opening two years ago, so he never got to see how successful the B&B would become.

Jen loved her partially round room. She had covered her walls with posters of sporting events and soccer stars, as well as a few cat pictures. Jen flopped on her bed, pulling Slinky close to her, and Zeke sat on the beanbag chair near the window.

"So who was talking to the truck driver?" Zeke asked once they were settled.

"I don't know, but I'll bet it was either Mr. Richards or Pierre."

Zeke nodded. "That makes sense, because I don't

think it was any of the bird-watchers. But what does his truck have to do with either of those men?"

"I can't figure that out," Jen admitted. "But if we're going to help the doomed circus in any way, we have to find out." She grinned. "And I have the perfect plan."

Zeke groaned.

✓͜

Early Saturday morning, Jen tapped on Zeke's door. "Ready?" she asked when he opened it.

He yawned. "I guess so." He glanced at his clock. It was after seven, but it felt a lot earlier.

"I told Aunt Bee we'd be leaving early to go to the circus," Jen said. "She said she didn't need help with the breakfast buffet today."

They coasted down the hill on their bikes. The morning mist was cool and smelled like the ocean. Waves crashing against the cliffs sounded muffled, and early gulls were out looking for a bite to eat.

They pedaled silently. Not a single car passed them. At last they rounded the corner where Tommy's uncle's garage sat. It was still dark enough that the outside security lights were on. But as they watched, the lights flickered off automatically one by one.

They parked their bikes on a side street, then

crept silently back to the garage. They had to finish what they were going to do before Burt officially opened the garage at eight.

"There it is," Jen whispered, pointing to the white truck in the mist.

Zeke nodded. They headed for the truck. Jen climbed onto the step by the driver's door and tried the handle. The door was locked. She jumped down while Zeke tried the other side.

"Rats," Jen said when they met at the rear of the truck. "How can we check it out if we can't get in?"

"Didn't you figure the truck would be locked?" Zeke asked.

Jen glared at him. "No. I didn't."

Zeke shook his head. "I should have known this wasn't the perfect plan." Just as the words were out of his mouth, he heard a creaking noise. He turned to find Jen slowly lifting the back door of the truck.

She grinned at him. "They didn't lock the back! Part of my plan, you know."

"Yeah, right."

Whether it was part of the plan or not, they were able to slide under the rolling door. The inside of the truck was dark.

"Can you see anything?" Jen asked.

Zeke squinted. "Not really. What's this all over the floor?"

He heard some rustling, then Jen said, "I think it's straw or hay."

"Look over here," Zeke said. In the shadowed light, they could make out two large, empty plastic bowls. "What are these for?"

Jen peered at the bowls then ran a piece of straw between her fingers. "I'll bet this truck is for the tiger."

Zeke was about to protest, but the more he thought about it, the more perfect it sounded. "That's right, because we saw it the morning the tiger was stolen."

"But it broke down," Jen continued. "So it wasn't there to take the tiger away."

"Then the tiger must still be in Mystic somewhere."

"But where? Whoever stole it couldn't have taken it too far away. They could have used one of the circus vans to take it somewhere, but those vans would be too small to take Lady very far. I know I wouldn't want a frightened tiger sitting in my backseat."

"Shhhh," Zeke suddenly hissed.

Jen heard voices. She recognized the deep voice of Burt, Tommy's uncle.

"I told you," Burt said, somewhere close by, "the truck will get done when it gets done."

"But I need it *now*."

"It's not ready *now*," Burt said.

The other man sighed in frustration. "When, then?"

"Come back at five-thirty today."

"That late?"

"If you keep wasting my time," Burt growled, "it won't be ready till Monday. I'm closed tomorrow."

"It had better be ready by five-thirty," the man threatened. "Or else!"

Out of Control

The voices faded away as Burt opened up his office. "Let's get out of here," Jen said.

The twins slipped under the truck door and quietly lowered it. Crouching, they hustled across the parking lot, dodging behind cars and trucks that were waiting to be repaired. Out of breath, they ran around the corner and jumped on their bikes. They didn't slow down until they were on Main Street. Delicious smells were wafting out of the Mystic Café.

"Let's get something to eat," Jen suggested. "It's too early to go to the circus, anyway."

Zeke agreed eagerly. Aunt Bee might be the best cook in town, but the Mystic Café was known for its honey buns, and Aunt Bee didn't even try to compete with them.

Inside the café, the twins sat in a window booth

and ordered fresh orange juice, a double order of honey buns for Zeke, and a toasted sesame bagel with veggie cream cheese for Jen.

While they waited for their order, they talked, keeping their voices down. The café filled up every morning, and they didn't want to be overheard.

Jen leaned forward, her elbows on the table. "So, if the truck is finished at five-thirty, and if it really is to transport the tiger, we're running out of time." She glanced at her watch. It was barely eight.

Zeke nodded. "We have to solve this case—*fast*."

"We know who the truck driver is, but even if we tell the police our suspicions, they're not going to be able to arrest him without proof."

"That's right. We need to find evidence."

"What we need to find is Lady," Jen said somberly.

"Right," Zeke agreed. "We know it must have something to do with a guest at the B&B because we saw the driver talking to someone."

"It had to be either Pierre or Mr. Richards," Jen reasoned. "The rest of the guests are part of a bird-watching organization. I'm sure they wouldn't want a tiger."

"But why would Pierre want to steal his own tiger?"

"What would Mr. Richards do with one?"

Their food arrived at that moment, and for a

while they were too busy eating to talk. When they finished, they decided it was still too early to go to the circus, so they headed down to the Mystic Marina. Zeke loved sailing and he enjoyed inspecting the yachts and sailboats tied up at the docks.

Some time later, Jen was surprised when she looked at her watch to find it was already ten o'clock. She called to Zeke, who was talking to the skipper of a 60-foot sailboat called the *Rakassa*.

Zeke waved to show he'd heard her, and a few minutes later he trotted over to where she was sitting on a piling, waiting for him. "Joe said he'd give me a tour of the *Rakassa* later," he said, beaming.

Jen rolled her eyes. She didn't like sailing—it made her seasick. "What about the case?" she asked. "We only have until five-thirty to solve it. You don't have time for a tour."

Zeke knew his sister was right. The most important thing right now was to find Lady and figure out who had stolen her. He took one last wistful look back at the beautiful sailing yacht. He wished he could spend all day sailing.

"Come on," Jen said, pulling him away.

They rode up Main Street, took a left on Fuller Road and then a right on School Street. The colorful circus was already noisy with music and it looked like all the rides were running. Winding between the crowds, Jen and Zeke kept their eyes open for anything that looked suspicious.

"Hi," said a boy about their age. He wore a red-and-white T-shirt and red shorts, and his brown hair was slicked back as though it were still wet.

"Hi," the twins responded, staring at him blankly.

The boy smiled at them. "What are you two up to?" He gestured with his right hand and in his left he balanced a coffee cake that was wrapped in a plastic bag.

Jen and Zeke glanced at each other. *Who was this kid? Did they know him from school?*

"Uh," Zeke said, "we're just, you know, checking out the rides."

"You have to try the Whoozy Doozy," the boy urged. Again he waved his right hand.

Suddenly, Jen laughed. "Mitchell!" she exclaimed.

The boy's eyes widened. "Huh?"

Now Zeke caught on, too. "Mitchell, we didn't recognize you at first," he admitted. "You look totally different without your clown makeup on."

Mitchell grinned. "You mean you didn't even know it was me?"

Jen shook her head. "Not until I recognized the way you wave your hands around when you talk.

We've never seen you without your wig and costume and makeup on."

Mitchell laughed. "I forgot about that. Hey, I'm taking this coffee cake over to Mr. Zambini's trailer. My mom made it because she feels bad about his accident. Mrs. Zambini said he's in their trailer, resting. Want to come along?"

Zeke shrugged. "Sure."

They followed Mitchell behind a roped-off area that had a sign reading RESTRICTED—CIRCUS PERSONNEL ONLY. Mitchell led them to a cluster of trailers. "This is where we live," Mitchell explained. "Pierre's trailer is over there, but I guess you know that." He waved in another direction. "I live down that way, and here's the Zambinis' trailer."

It wasn't hard to miss. It was painted a dark purple and gold letters spelled out ZAMBINI across the side. Mitchell knocked on the door. No one answered.

"Maybe he fell asleep," Jen suggested.

"Maybe," Mitchell agreed. He tried the door handle. It turned. "Let's just leave this inside on the kitchen table. We don't have to wake him up."

They entered the trailer, tiptoeing and not speaking. Jen was amazed to see how much could fit into such a small space. There was a kitchen with a sink, refrigerator, stove, and oven, an eating area, and a living room with plush green carpeting on the floor. The bathroom door stood open, and two other doors farther down were open, too.

"The bedrooms are down there," Mitchell mouthed and pointed as he put the cake on the table.

Jen turned around and glanced down at the counter, which was covered with piles of opened letters. She noticed that the envelopes were holding what looked like bills. One pink sheet stuck out of an envelope and Jen could read the words "Final notice" written across the top in bold letters. Feeling guilty for spying, she moved toward the door.

Zeke stepped after her, then noticed the vase of flowers on the side table with a "Get well soon" card attached. One of the flowers in the arrangement was a lily. He tried to step away from the flowers as quickly as possible, but it was too late. His nose itched. Lilies always made him sneeze. He tried to squeeze his nostrils closed to stop the tickle, but it didn't work. A squeaky sneeze erupted. The three of them stared at one another, expecting Mr. Zambini to come groggily out of his bedroom at any second. But nothing happened.

"Either he's a deep sleeper," Zeke said with a sniffle, "or he's not here."

"Either way, we'd better get out of here," Jen said.

She led the way out of the trailer.

"I've got a while before I have to get into costume," Mitchell said. "Let's go on the Whoozy Doozy,
my treat."

"Sure," Zeke said. One ride wouldn't hurt, but

then they had to get down to some serious sleuthing. Five-thirty would be here before they knew it.

Jen made a face. If sailboats made her feel ill, she could just imagine what the Whoozy Doozy would do.

The Whoozy Doozy line was long. The young man with the droopy blond mustache who was running the ride said that the regular ride operator was sick this morning and it had taken a while to find a replacement. He let Mitchell cut to the front of the line and they all got to ride for free. They strapped themselves into a small compartment just in time for the ride to start. The ride whirled slowly at first. Jen grinned. This wasn't so bad after all. But then the ride twirled faster and faster. Not only was the compartment going in circles, but the whole ride was turning as well. Jen began to feel green. She could see that Zeke and Mitchell were having the time of their lives, though. The ride continued spinning faster and faster. Jen closed her eyes, praying the ride would end soon. But it didn't. If anything, it seemed to turn even faster. And now it was bumping up and down, too.

She forced her eyes open and fear shot through her—not because Zeke was turning green, too, but because of the terrified look on Mitchell's face.

Something was definitely wrong!

"The ride is out of control!" Mitchell shouted.

10
The Million Dollar Question

Jen knew she'd pass out if the ride didn't slow down. Along with the whirling and bumping, there was now a loud banging sound. *What if the operator couldn't ever stop the ride? They'd be twirling around forever!*

Even as these thoughts careened through her head, the noise and bumping abruptly stopped. Slowly, the spinning decreased, but it seemed like it took forever. As soon as the ride stopped, Mitchell released the strap that held them in place.

"I wonder what happened," he said, shaking his head to clear the dizziness.

Jen scrambled off the ride. Her legs wobbled and for a second she thought she'd fall flat on her face.

Zeke grabbed her arm to keep her on her feet. They passed the ride operator, who was inspecting the gears of the ride with two men in gray jumpsuits.

"Those are the circus mechanics," Mitchell told them as they walked by.

One of the mechanics scratched his head and said, "Looks like someone purposely jammed this gear."

Jen pulled Zeke aside. "Did you hear that?"

Zeke nodded. "Another act of sabotage."

Mitchell said he had to go put his clown makeup on and waved good-bye. As he trotted off, Jen and Zeke continued their conversation.

"But why would someone want to sabotage a ride?" Jen mused.

"So far there has been the Zambini accident," Zeke began, lifting one finger. He lifted another one. "And painting Pierre's trailer."

"Stealing Lady," Jen added. "And don't forget the clown noses and the stake in the ostrich cage."

"And now this ride." Zeke shook his head. "It doesn't seem to add up. Let's go home. I have a theory and there's something I want to look up on the Internet."

As soon as they got back to the B&B, the twins searched for Aunt Bee to tell her they were home.

As they neared the parlor, Zeke put his finger to

his lips. Jen heard someone talking—she recognized Mr. Richards's voice. The twins tiptoed so they wouldn't disturb him. Aunt Bee always reminded them that it was crucial to let the guests feel as if they were in their own homes and could talk on the phone without being disturbed, or even take a nap in the parlor if they wanted to.

Mr. Richards looked up at them and grinned. "Late this afternoon," he said into the receiver. "Don't worry." With that, he hung up, his diamond pinky ring flashing brilliantly. "What are you kids up to?"

Zeke shrugged. "Just looking for our aunt."

"Slinky, cut that out," Jen said as her Maine coon cat purred and rubbed against Mr. Richards's dark blue suit. She didn't normally warm up to the guests so quickly.

Mr. Richards laughed. "It's quite all right. I love cats and I miss all of mine." He rubbed Slinky's head and the cat purred even louder.

The three of them laughed.

"I think your aunt said she was going for a walk," Mr. Richards said.

Jen knew her aunt loved to walk along the bluff with the salty ocean breeze blowing her long gray hair. She could be gone for an hour or more. The twins excused themselves and hustled upstairs to

Zeke's room. He booted up his computer and signed onto the Web.

"What are you looking for?" Jen asked, flopping on a chair she had pulled up next to Zeke's. Her legs still felt a little wobbly from the ride.

"I memorized the license plate number on the truck. I just want to see if I can trace it."

Jen could hardly keep up with Zeke's fingers flashing over the keyboard and the way he flicked his mouse around. After ten minutes of investigating, Zeke sat back with a grin. "Check out this new Web site. It searches license plates for free, and it only takes seconds. . . ."

Jen leaned forward, anticipation tingling her fingers and toes. "So? Who does the truck belong to?"

Zeke put up his hand. "Just a sec. The computer is still searching."

They stared at the screen. Finally, a new image appeared. It listed the license plate number, the state in which it was registered, and the owner's name.

"The Pyramid Group?" Jen read out loud. "What's that?"

Zeke frowned. "It's the company that owns the truck. That must be why there's a black triangle painted on the side of it." His fingers flew over the keyboard again. He sat back in defeat. "The Pyramid Group must be the only company in the world that doesn't have a Web site. So we can't even find out anything about it or who the owners are."

Jen groaned. "A dead end."

"Hopefully not for Lady," Zeke said grimly, working at the keyboard again. "Let's look up the Big Top Insurance Company. I remember Pierre mentioning it."

They easily found the site and read the description of the company. "Insurance for all amusements, large and small. Put your trust in us. You lose, we pay!"

"It must be Pierre's insurance company," Jen said. "I wonder if he gets money for losing Lady?"

With Jen looking over his shoulder, he clicked on a policy information icon. They both read silently.

Then Zeke whistled. "The policy for rare animals covers up to a million dollars," he breathed.

Jen felt stunned. "That sure gives Pierre a motive for stealing Lady. It would take him months, if not years, of performing to make that much money from ticket sales. All he has to do is get rid of Lady and collect the insurance money and he's got it made."

Zeke thought for a moment and frowned. "But we still haven't figured out what all those other accidents and vandalism have to do with Lady's disappearance."

"Maybe he's trying to collect insurance on everything bad that happens?"

"That doesn't make sense. If he's trying to get the insurance company to pay for Lady, he wouldn't want to jeopardize that by having too many accidents happen or the insurance company might cancel the policy."

Jen nodded. Zeke had a point. "And it doesn't explain the clown footprint we found in the cage. When the tiger was stolen, Pierre was having a fit over his painted trailer."

They were both silent for a long moment, trying to sort out the clues.

"It'd be best if we could just find Lady," she said as she stood up. "Come on, we have to go look for her. If we find her we'll know who took her."

They hurried down the spiral staircase of the lighthouse tower, then stopped in the kitchen and grabbed sandwiches for lunch. Jen had one idea of where to look for Lady. She told Zeke about it once they were on their bikes and heading for town again.

"The old haunted house on Front Street would be the perfect place to hide a tiger," Jen insisted. "No one goes near that spooky place."

"But someone would hear if Lady roared."

"Well, it's worth a shot."

When they got to town, they headed for Front Street and rode south until they reached number 502, the old Murray mansion. They stood out front and stared up at the pointy roof peaks, the crumbling roof tiles, the broken and missing window shutters, and the peeling gray paint.

Jen shivered. Maybe this wasn't such a good idea after all.

Zeke took a deep breath. "Let's go," he said, sounding a lot braver than he felt.

They left their bikes on the pavement and passed through the creaking front gate. As soon as they walked onto the property, the sun went behind a cloud and everything became even gloomier. The front stairs groaned as they walked up them to the sagging front porch. A broken porch swing swayed in the breeze, one side of it still bolted to the ceiling of the porch.

"Think this is safe?" Zeke asked.

"No," Jen admitted. "But we have to find Lady before it's too late."

The front door was missing, so it was easy to enter the house. The high ceilings and dusty, dark drapes over the windows made Jen feel like she was entering a cave. It took a moment for their eyes to adjust.

Above them something creaked.

Zeke's heart slammed against his ribs. "What was that?" he hissed.

They heard another creak, followed by a loud thump.

Wide-eyed, Jen turned to Zeke. "It's either Lady or a ghost," she said with a gulp.

11

Haunted?

The twins cocked their heads, straining to hear.

"We have to go look," Jen whispered after a few seconds of absolute silence. She headed for the wide staircase that led up into the darkness of the second floor. They climbed slowly, watching and listening the whole way. On the second floor landing, they stopped and listened.

Zeke heard a shuffling sound down the hall to the left. He pointed. Jen nodded, and they headed in that direction. What if they came face-to-face with a hungry tiger? She gritted her teeth and kept moving. Now she could hear the noise again. It was getting louder.

Suddenly, Jen stepped on a loose floorboard. It screeched like a frightened cat, sending chills from Jen's toes to the top of her head.

"Nice going," Zeke whispered.

The shuffling sound stopped. Then they heard the sound of running feet. Jen and Zeke rushed down the hall. It zigzagged, then led to a second set of stairs heading down. Before they started down the stairs, they heard a bang below them.

Jen ran to one of the tall, dusty windows and peered out into the backyard. She gasped. "It's Mrs. Watson!"

The twins watched as their science teacher ran across the yard and scrambled through a gap in the back fence. Mrs. Watson took one last frightened look back at the mansion before disappearing from view.

"I wonder what she was doing here?" Jen said.

"She's been snooping around a lot," Zeke said. "She must be up to something."

They searched the rest of the house, but they didn't find Lady, or any ghosts, much to their relief.

Outside, it took a few minutes for their eyes to get used to the bright sunlight. When they could see again, they rode up and down every street, keeping their eyes open for any likely hiding place for Lady.

Jen gave a sigh of disgust as they reached Main Street. "Maybe we're completely wrong about what's going on. Maybe Lady really did escape on her own and the truck is for transporting goats or something."

Zeke gave his sister a look. "Are you kidding?

We've pieced the clues together perfectly so far. Everything makes sense."

They passed the Mystic Café on their left. Then they rode by the self-serve laundry and the Smith Sisters' Salon. Just after they crossed Front Street, Zeke whistled with appreciation. Mr. Richards's awesome roadster was parked in front of Perfect Pets. It gleamed in the bright sunlight. He had to stop and admire it close up.

"That is so great," Zeke said with longing.

"Yeah, and you only need, like, a million dollars to get your own," Jen said dryly. She looked around. "I wonder where he is?" Then she spotted him in Perfect Pets. "Let's see what he's buying."

They leaned their bikes against the wall, and stepped inside the store. Several people were in the store looking at the Persian kittens. One boy was begging his father for a pug. Mr. Richards stood near the counter with a large, bright blue-and-yellow bird on his arm.

"Nice parrot," Zeke said, walking up to him.

Mr. Richards turned and smiled at the twins. "It's a macaw. I've never seen one with such a beautiful blend of colors and such bright eyes."

As though the bird knew they were talking about him, he bobbed his head and squawked loudly.

Jen laughed. "He sure is a noisy guy."

"Oh, that's nothing," Mr. Richards said. "When you get thirty birds together in one aviary, now *that's* noisy!"

"Thirty of these guys?" Zeke asked.

Mr. Richards nodded. "I can't seem to stop buying them. My menagerie just keeps growing." He paid for the bird, then asked the twins if they needed a ride back to the B&B.

Zeke groaned. "I can't, I have my bike here."

"Maybe some other time, then. See you later," Mr. Richards said.

Jen and Zeke followed him out of the store and watched him pack the birdcage onto the passenger seat and zoom off.

Jen sighed. "We may as well head home, too. We haven't found out anything more and we're running out of time."

"We need to make suspect sheets," Zeke said. "It's the only way to sort everything and *everyone* out."

Back at the B&B, the twins settled themselves in Zeke's room. Jen grabbed a couple of pens and several sheets of paper and started writing.

Mystic Lighthouse

Suspect Sheet

Name: PIERRE THE MAGNIFICENT

Motive: TRYING TO MAKE HIS SHOW BIGGER AND BETTER; INSURANCE MONEY?

Clues: Why would he want to steal the star of the show? Is it worth it?

WAS HE THE ONE TALKING TO THE TRUCK DRIVER?

THE TIGER WAS PROBABLY INSURED. MAYBE PIERRE WOULD RATHER HAVE THE INSURANCE MONEY TO UPGRADE THE SHOW?

What did he mean by telling Terra he was counting on her and why did that make her upset? Counting on her to steal the tiger?

Was the tiger stolen while he was distracting everyone with his ruined trailer? Is he working with someone?

Mystic Lighthouse

Suspect Sheet

Name: Mrs. Watson

Motive: Hates to see the tiger in captivity

Clues: Admitted she's against animals in captivity and says she'd do ANYTHING to let the tiger go free.

WHY WAS SHE SNEAKING AROUND THE SHOW AND NEAR THE TIGER CAGE? TO LET THE TIGER OUT?

WHAT WAS SHE DOING AT THE MURRAY MANSION?

Mystic Lighthouse

Suspect Sheet

Name: Terra the Tiger Trainer

Motive: Working with Pierre?

Clues: What was she talking to Pierre about after the trapeze accident? What did she mean by "You can trust me?" Trust her to steal the tiger? And what money was she talking about?

SHE WAS A CRYING WRECK AFTER TIGER DISAPPEARED—WAS SHE FAKING IT TO THROW OFF SUSPICION?

Was her key to Lady's cage really stolen or was she just trying to make it look like someone else could have done it?

Mystic Lighthouse

Suspect Sheet

Name: Mr. Richards

Motive: He collects exotic birds, could he collect other exotic animals, too?

Clues: WHY IS HE LURKING AROUND THE CIRCUS? WHAT CONNECTION DOES HE HAVE?

He admits he loves cats. Could he want a tiger? But he was on the phone all morning when the tiger was stolen.

Who is he talking to on the phone all the time?

HE TRAVELS ALL AROUND THE WORLD AND HAS BEEN TO SIBERIA. THE MISSING TIGER IS A SIBERIAN TIGER. ANY CONNECTION?

Mystic Lighthouse

Suspect Sheet

Name: Zambini the Great

Motive: Mad at Pierre for replacing the Great Zambini act with a tiger?

Clues: Who cut their trapeze rope?

Where was Mr. Zambini when he was supposed to be in his trailer resting?

Did he really hurt his leg, or was he faking it so he wouldn't have to perform? But why?

When the twins finished, they shuffled through the sheets again and again, but nothing seemed to sort itself out.

"Have we missed something?" Jen wondered out loud.

Zeke checked the clock on his desk. "I don't know, but we're running out of time!"

Note to Reader

Have you figured out who stole Lady? Is it the same person who is causing all the accidents at the circus?

If you review this case carefully, you'll discover important clues that Jen and Zeke have missed along the way.

Take your time. Carefully review your suspect sheets. When you think you have a solution, read the last chapter to find out if Jen and Zeke can put all the pieces together to solve *The Mystery of the Missing Tiger*.

Good luck!

Solution

Another Mystery Solved!

"It's five o'clock!" Zeke said. "The truck will be ready at five-thirty."

"Think!" Jen commanded.

"I *am* thinking," Zeke protested. He looked over the suspect sheets again. Something was niggling at the back of his mind. Something they hadn't written down on the suspect sheets. . . . Mr. Richards's ring!

"What?" Jen asked, sensing her brother's growing excitement.

"The Pyramid Group owns the truck, right?"

Jen nodded.

"Well, Mr. Richards wears a diamond pinky ring in the shape of a pyramid!"

Jen frowned. "That's not exactly solid evidence."

"Think about how he travels all over the world. He loves animals, right? He *collects* them."

Slowly, Jen nodded. "And he loved Slinky, even though she was leaving cat hairs all over his expensive clothes. And he sure is rich enough to buy a Siberian tiger."

"Exactly," Zeke agreed. "Tigers are so rare that if he couldn't find someone to sell him one, he'd have to steal it!"

Suddenly, Jen frowned. "But he couldn't have stolen Lady. He was on the phone all Friday morning, remember?"

For a moment, Zeke paused. Then he snapped his fingers. "He must have someone on the inside working for him. One of the clowns must be his partner. Which one? Who needs the money?"

Jen closed her eyes and thought about the clown clues. Which clown? Mitchell had said he didn't think any of the clowns would do it. And the shoes with the blue paint on them belonged to . . . no one.

"It's not a clown," Jen said finally.

"But what about the clown footprint?"

"It was an old costume. And remember how hard it was to recognize Mitchell without his makeup on? I only recognized him by the way he moved his arms around when he talked. Someone was wearing the clown suit as a disguise."

Something flashed in Zeke's head. "I saw a

clown," he said slowly, "on the morning Lady was stolen. I thought it was weird that he was in his costume already since none of the others were. He walked with a limp."

"*What* did you say?" Jen demanded.

"I saw a clown—"

"Did you say he limped?"

"Uh, yeah."

"Who is the only performer in the circus with a limp?"

Then it dawned on Zeke. "Mr. Zambini!"

Nervously he checked the clock again—5:07.

Jen also looked at the clock, then she jumped up and headed for the door.

"Where are you going?" Zeke called.

She motioned for him to follow her. As they raced down the stairs, she hurriedly told Zeke her plan between breaths. "The truck. We have to sneak into the back. It'll go pick up Lady. We'll find Lady. It's the only way—we'll get to her—before they get her out of town."

Zeke grabbed Jen's arm and hauled her to a stop. "Are you nuts?" he demanded.

"Do you have a better idea?" Jen asked, moving on again.

Zeke fumed. No, he didn't have a better idea, but

he didn't exactly want to be eaten by a tiger, either. On the spur of the moment, he stopped at the bee-hive-shaped kitchen phone.

"What are you doing?" Jen asked. "We don't have time for phone calls."

Zeke motioned for his sister to hang on for one second as he dialed Tommy's number. Busy. He tried again. Still busy. He tried Stacey's number and she picked up on the second ring.

Tripping over his words, Zeke tried to explain what was going on. "You need to find Pierre and call the police. Then get them to follow the truck that's at Tommy's uncle's garage. The one with the black triangle on the side. Tell Pierre it will lead everyone to the missing tiger!"

Stacey started to ask questions, but Zeke knew she could talk forever if he let her. "Just get going," he interrupted. "It could be a matter of life or death." *Ours*, he thought as he slammed the phone down and dashed after Jen.

With her wavy brown hair flying out behind her, Jen zoomed down the hill and headed for the garage, pedaling like crazy. They hoped the truck wouldn't have been picked up already.

As they rounded the corner, Jen sighed with relief. The truck was still there! The twins ditched their bikes and ran toward the truck, hunching down in hopes that no one would notice them. Zeke couldn't breathe until they had managed to lift the back door a crack and slip into the dark truck. When they slid the door back down, they were left in complete blackness.

Zeke breathed with relief.

"I hope the driver won't check back here before he takes off," Jen said, positioning herself against the wall so she wouldn't roll around when the truck started moving.

Zeke groaned. "Great. I never thought of that. And what are we going to do when they open the door to let Lady in? They're not going to be too thrilled to see us here."

"Don't worry. Stacey will call the police."

At that moment, the truck rumbled to life. Jen braced herself as the driver backed up and took a left out of the driveway. She tried to imagine where they were heading, but after several rights and lefts, she got lost.

Suddenly, the truck lurched to the right and Jen hit her head against the side as they bumped over a rough road before coming to a jerky stop. The motor cut off.

Jen froze. All of a sudden this did not seem like a great plan. She heard voices outside. Someone grabbed the handle of the back door and lifted. With a loud rattle, it flew up. Jen and Zeke stared right into the eyes of Mr. Richards and Mr. Zambini.

Zeke looked beyond the two angry men, but no police were in sight. They were doomed!

Jen recognized where they were right away. *Of course!* she thought. *The old, abandoned ballfield.* A dreadful thought was sinking in. What if the police hadn't followed the truck? Would anyone think to look for them here?

"What are you two doing in there?" Mr. Richards demanded.

"I—we—" Zeke began.

"We know everything," Jen blurted out, raising her voice to compete with the crashing waves nearby. "And you're not going to get away with it."

A slow smile spread across Mr. Richards's face. He smoothed one hand over his oiled hair. "Of course I am. I always do. How do you think I have collected so many exotic creatures for my menagerie?"

Mr. Zambini stood nervously at his side.

Then Mr. Richards's smile turned nasty. "Go get Lady," he ordered.

Mr. Zambini blanched. "What about the kids?"

"Exactly," Mr. Richards said. "We'll find out if Lady has any wild instincts left in her."

Jen gasped.

"You're going to be in big trouble for this," Zeke said boldly.

Jen looked at her twin in amazement. He sounded so sure of himself. Then the faint sound that Zeke had obviously already heard reached her ears. Sirens!

Very soon, Mr. Richards and Mr. Zambini also heard the sirens, but it was too late for them to escape. Two police cars zoomed down the dirt road and slammed to a stop, surrounding them. Right behind them a circus van kicked up dust as it stopped and Pierre, Stacey, Mrs. Watson, and Terra jumped out. The police immediately put handcuffs on Mr. Richards, Mr. Zambini, and the truck driver.

"You have a lot of explaining to do," one of the police officers growled.

"We can explain most of it," Jen offered. She told everyone how they had figured out all the clues and discovered who was behind Lady's cat-nabbing. She looked around. "But we didn't figure out that this old abandoned sports field would be such a great hiding place. It makes sense. No one comes here now that there's a brand-new field, so no one would see Lady, and the Atlantic covers up most sounds."

Zeke turned to Terra, who now had possession of Lady's leash. The immense tiger lay down patiently at her feet. "We thought you might be guilty," he admitted.

Terra's green eyes opened wide. "Me? Why?"

"We heard you arguing with Pierre, promising him money."

Terra smiled. "I was promising to make him money with Lady." She bent down and scratched the tiger's ears. "We make quite a team."

"The circus wasn't doing well," Pierre said. "I needed a new act to revive ticket sales. I was nervous that Terra's act wouldn't do it," he said sheepishly. "I'm afraid I was rather on edge and not very kind."

Jen faced Mr. Zambini. "You were the one who stole Terra's keys for the cage, right?"

Mr. Zambini nodded, not lifting his face to look at anyone.

"You were that jealous of the new act that you wanted to get rid of it?" Zeke asked.

"No, no," Mr. Zambini protested in his slight accent. "I needed the money for my son. He is in medical school and the cost is very high. He wanted to be a veterinarian. It was his dream and I wished it to come true. But I couldn't afford it. When someone told me Mr. Richards would pay one hundred thousand dollars for the tiger, I made my plans."

"You cut your own rope," Jen guessed out loud.

"And caused all the little problems like missing clown costumes and painting Pierre's trailer blue."

"Yes," Mr. Zambini admitted. "I thought if there were many things going wrong, and one of them happened to me, no one could suspect me. They would just think someone was trying to ruin the circus."

Jen and Zeke glanced at each other. "It worked," Jen admitted. "It wasn't until Zeke remembered seeing a clown who walked with a limp that we figured out it was you."

Zeke turned to Mr. Richards. "And we thought you were a banker."

"Why a banker?" Mr. Richards asked.

"We heard you talking about bucks," Jen said. "You said the more bucks the better."

Mr. Richards frowned. "I was talking about male rabbits."

Jen shook her head. "Rabbits?"

"A buck is a male rabbit. My supplier found several bucks with extremely unusual markings. I wanted them for my collection."

"What do you do with all your animals anyway?" Stacey asked. Jen noticed that her best friend had her pen and pad of paper out.

Mr. Richards shrugged. "Not much. I just collect them."

"Like a zoo?" Stacey persisted.

"A *private* zoo," Mr. Richards said. "I don't like anyone else looking at my animals."

"I think we've heard enough," the police officer said. He pulled on Mr. Richards's arm. "You three are under arrest. You're coming with us."

After they left, Jen looked at her science teacher. "What are you doing here?"

Mrs. Watson looked embarrassed. "I was at the circus to see if Lady had been found when the call came. I just jumped in the van before anyone could say anything, and here I am. I had to be sure Lady was safe."

"But why were you at the old Murray mansion?" Zeke asked. "We saw you there."

"That was you?" Mrs. Watson exclaimed. She laughed. "You scared the daylights out of me. Like you, I was searching for the tiger. I was afraid she was being abused."

Terra clucked her tongue. "I've examined Lady, and she's in perfect health. The robbers didn't hurt her, thank goodness."

Lady rubbed her massive head against Terra's legs. "Yes, I missed you too," Terra said with a laugh.

Mrs. Watson sighed. "It seems that Lady really likes you."

"Of course," Terra said. "I raised her from a cub,

saving her from terrible people who were trying to illegally raise white tigers for their pelts."

"How horrible," Mrs. Watson said. "I guess she really is better off with you. I'm sorry I made such a fuss."

Terra waved away her apology. "I understand. And believe me, I treat Lady like a *queen*."

Stacey moved closer to the tiger trainer. "Can you tell me where you were born?"

Terra looked confused. "What does that have to do with anything?"

"It's background for the article I'm writing," Stacey explained, holding her pen poised above the paper.

"Always looking for a front page story," Jen said with a chuckle.

"Let's go to the circus," Zeke said. "With everything going on, we haven't had a chance to really enjoy it."

"We can look for Tommy," Jen said.

Stacey grinned. "Not that we'll have to look very hard."

"He'll be at the food stand," Jen and Zeke chimed in together. Then they burst out laughing.

About the Author

Laura E. Williams has written more than twenty-five books for children, her most recent being the books in the Mystic Lighthouse Mysteries series, *ABC Kids*, and *The Executioner's Daughter*. In her spare time she works on the rubber art stamp company that she started in her garage.

Ms. Williams loves lighthouses. Someday she hopes to visit a lighthouse bed-and-breakfast just like the one in Mystic, Maine.

Mystic Lighthouse

Suspect Sheet

Name:

Motive:

Clues: